# CHOOSE YOUR OWN ADVENTURE®

# TERROR ON THE *TITANIC*

## BY JIM WALLACE

## ILLUSTRATED BY FRANK BOLLE

*An R. A. Montgomery Book*

BANTAM BOOKS
NEW YORK • TORONTO • LONDON • SYDNEY • AUCKLAND

For Michael Lamb and Ian.

RL4, age 008–012

TERROR ON THE *TITANIC*
*A Bantam Book / August 1997*

*CHOOSE YOUR OWN ADVENTURE® is a registered*
*trademark of Bantam Books,*
*a division of Bantam Doubleday Dell Publishing Group, Inc.*
*Registered in U.S. Patent and Trademark Office and elsewhere.*

*Original conception of Edward Packard.*

*Cover art by Samson Pollen.*
*Interior illustrations by Frank Bolle.*

ISBN 0-553-48650-0

*Published simultaneously in the United States and Canada*

Bantam Books are published by Bantam Books, a division of
Bantam Doubleday Dell Publishing Group, Inc. Its trademark,
consisting of the words "Bantam Books" and the portrayal of a
rooster, is Registered in U.S. Patent and Trademark Office and
in other countries. Marca Registrada. Bantam Books, 1540
Broadway, New York, New York 10036.

PRINTED IN THE UNITED STATES OF AMERICA

OPM      0  9  8  7  6  5  4  3  2

# Glossary of Ship's Terms

**Abovedecks**—On the top deck of a ship, in the open.

**Aft**—Toward or at the rear of a ship.

**Amidships**—Toward or at the middle of a ship.

**Bow**—The front of a ship.

**Bridge**—An enclosed platform above the main deck in the front of a ship. From here the captain or his officers control and steer the ship.

**Broadside**—Sideways movement of a ship. Also, the side of a ship above the waterline.

**Bulkhead**—Any wall or partition on a ship.

**Capstan**—A winch mounted vertically on the deck of a ship. Used for pulling docking lines or anchor chains.

**Crow's nest**—A lookout platform on the foremast (front mast) of a ship.

**Davits**—Sets of small cranes mounted near lifeboats to lower or raise them.

**Fore**—Toward or at the front of a ship.

**Forecastle**—Top deck of a ship in front of the bridge; the deck nearest the bow.

**Helm**—The wheel that steers a ship.

**Poop deck**—Small top deck in the stern of a ship, above the main stern deck.

**Port**—The left side of a ship.

**Promenade deck**—An upper deck for first-class passengers, open toward the stern and covered near the bow.

**Quartermaster**—A ship's officer who operates the ship's helm.

**Starboard**—The right side of a ship.

**Stern**—The rear of a ship.

**Well deck**—An open deck that sits lower than the main deck, located in both the stern and the bow.

DAVITS    PROMENADE DECK    FORE WELL DECK    BRIDGE    CROWSNEST

POOP DECK

AFT WELL DECK

STERN                     BOW

White Star Line
Three Screw Royal Mail Steamship
**TITANIC**
March 31, 1909 · April 15, 1912

# WARNING!!!

Do not read this book straight through from beginning to end. These pages contain many different adventures you may have as a passenger on board the great luxury ship the *Titanic* when it hits an iceberg during its very first voyage.

From time to time as you read along, you'll have a chance to make a choice. The adventures you have are the results of your choices. You are responsible because you choose. After you make a decision, follow the directions to find out what happens to you next.

Think carefully before you decide what to do in this dangerous situation. Each move you make determines whether you will live to return home and tell your story to the newspapers, or die an icy death in the waters of the Atlantic. Not just your own life but the lives of other passengers are in your hands. You'd better act quickly—who knows how long before the *Titanic* sinks to the bottom of the ocean?

Good luck!

You stand on the deck of the RMS *Titanic,* the brand-new White Star ocean liner. She's the biggest, most luxurious ship in the world, and she's on her first voyage across the ocean, from Southampton, England, to New York City. The date is April 10, 1912.

The ship has just pulled away from Southampton quay and is moving into the Test River. A huge crowd walks along the quay, following the great ship's progress down the narrow river channel.

The *Titanic* glides by the *New York,* a smaller ocean liner moored at the side of the river. You watch as the smaller ship is sucked toward the *Titanic. Bang! Bang! Bang!* You hear several loud reports, like gunshots. Looking down, you see the ropes holding the moored ship arc high into the air. They must have snapped! The *New York* begins to swing away from her mooring directly toward the *Titanic!*

You gasp and grasp the railing tightly, expecting at any minute to feel a shuddering impact. As you watch, the *Titanic* slows to a stop, and the bow of the *New York* swings past her port side. A collision is narrowly avoided.

"That was a close one," says a tall, gaunt man standing next to you. He has a pale, lined face with a thin, grim mouth. He speaks with a lilting Scottish accent. "It's a bad way to begin a maiden voyage. A bad omen."

*Turn to page 2.*

# 2

"Bad omen! Pah!" says a middle-aged Englishman standing nearby. A watch chain hangs from the brocade waistcoat buttoned tightly round his stout middle. He sports great gray muttonchop whiskers. "There's nothing to fear! The technical journals I've read say she's unsinkable. She's a wonder ship!"

"Aye," sighs the tall man knowingly. "She is indeed a wonder ship, a mighty ship. But the ocean is mightier still. Many a mighty ship has kissed the bottom of the sea." With that, the man turns and walks slowly away.

"Don't listen to him," says the Englishman. "This ship is beautifully engineered. I tell you, she *can't* sink."

*Go on to the next page.*

"She is big and beautiful," you say, glancing around admiringly. The *Titanic* is nine hundred feet long and has four huge funnels. Her hull is painted a shiny black and her deck superstructure is white; her yellow funnels with black tips rise sixty feet above her top deck. It does seem unbelievable that such a massive ship could sink to the bottom of the ocean. Still, the Scotsman's comment has chilled you.

"Oh, so you're an American!" says the Englishman. He extends his hand. "The name is Hardcastle. Were you on holiday in England?"

"No," you say, shaking his hand. "I've been in London for the past month, studying classical piano."

*Go on to page 4.*

**4**

"A classical pianist, eh?" says Mr. Hardcastle. "So you've been in England alone, then?"

"No. My father was with me. He has an import-export business. He had to stay in London to meet a client. I'm returning to New York with his partner."

"Import-export business, you say. Would the name of your father's partner be Andrew Tempkin?" asks Mr. Hardcastle. You nod. "Yes, I met the chap just before we boarded. He told me he bought himself a black Rolls-Royce."

"Yes—it's on board. He's taking it back to New York," you say.

"You know, you should meet my son, Jack," says Mr. Hardcastle. "He's just your age and a very agreeable lad. I'm sure the two of you will get along famously."

*Go on to the next page.*

Mr. Hardcastle's mention of Andrew gets you thinking about him and the gold Buddha statues that he and your father imported from Siam. The box containing the statues arrived at the office in London while your father was out, and Andrew refused to open it in your presence. He made you run out on an errand. When you came back, your father had returned, and he and Andrew were examining the two statues, each about a foot high. Your father was disappointed. The workmanship was poor. Worse, the statues weren't solid gold but made of lead painted with gold leaf. Your father was angry and vowed he'd get even with the Siamese trader who cheated him.

Andrew supported your father and agreed the trader was a scoundrel. But something about his manner made you suspicious. In contrast to your father's genuine rage, Andrew's reaction seemed mild. You don't trust him, and you aren't happy to be sharing this transatlantic journey with him.

*Turn to page 11.*

# 6

The Marconi Room, the "radio shack," is up forward on the port, or left, side of the ship. To get there you walk along the deck to the other end of the ship. You and Jack shiver in the arctic air. Overhead the night sky blazes with stars; below, the ocean is glassy smooth. You're amazed at how calm the water is. There's not a ripple.

Yesterday afternoon Harold, one of the two radio operators, met you as he was leaving the shack. He invited you to drop by anytime. Without knocking, you open the door and go in, Jack behind you. A hot smell of electrical insulation hangs in the air. A man is on duty, but it's not Harold.

"Mind if we watch a minute?" you ask.

The operator doesn't hear you, or if he does, he's too busy to reply. He's wearing earphones and staring intently at a stack of papers. A blue spark flashes between the contacts of the radio telegraph key he's tapping with his index finger. You're entranced by the rhythmic Morse code and the sparking light. The message sounds important, but you can't understand it.

Jack does, though. You watch him concentrate on the pulsing beeps as you both stand nervously just inside the door.

*Go on to the next page.*

Suddenly an incoming signal blares from the earphones so loudly you can hear it across the room. The operator tears the earphones from his head and smacks the stack of paper. With an exasperated look, he raps back a message. He spots you and says, "Not now, too busy. Later. Out, please."

You both nod and duck out the door. Jack grabs your arm. "That was weird. Those were private messages he was sending, maybe to a land station for relaying. Messages like 'Meet you Wednesday noon at the Waldorf Astoria.' Then a signal came in. He got flustered and told the guy to shut up and keep the air clear. Another ship must be nearby."

"What was the other ship saying?" you ask.

"I couldn't get the first part. Something like 'stopped, surrounded by ice,' " Jack says.

"Ice! Icebergs!" you say. "Maybe we're coming into an ice field. Let's go on deck. We may be able to spot some."

"Icebergs! Who cares? I'd rather go visit my friend the chief baker," says Jack. "He's baking bread right now for tomorrow. He'd give us a loaf. Think of it—hot, fresh bread . . ."

"Oh, come on, be a good sport! Let's see if we can spot a few icebergs, then we'll warm up at the baker's," you say. Jack reluctantly agrees. "I'll get the binoculars and meet you on the promenade deck," you add.

*Turn to page 15.*

# 8

You hang on underwater, stars flashing behind your eyes from the icy shock of the water over your head.

Something lets go with a ripping vibration. The raft pops up to the surface with you clinging to it. You're thirty feet from the *Titanic*'s stern, finally clear of it as it glides below the surface.

A weak voice calls to you. It's McCracken. You drag his body onto the raft. He can't talk. After a while he just lies still.

Other people struggle to climb on the raft. You're too numb and weak to help them much. Most of those who succeed lie motionless like McCracken.

As dawn breaks, you notice a ship far in the distance pulling up people from the *Titanic*'s lifeboats. A few hours later, another ship steams slowly back and forth through the bits and pieces of the *Titanic*'s wreckage.

She's so close you can almost make out her name. You try yelling, but your voice is too weak to carry. When you try to stand and wave your arms, you stumble and fall into the water. It takes precious minutes and all your strength to regain the raft. By then the ship has begun to steam away.

## The End

# 10

You're still angry about the brush-off—that and the man's arrogant and patronizing manner. You don't trust him. Andrew makes you uneasy too. You don't understand why your father chose him as a partner. Sure, he's sharp in business, a real smooth operator. But that's the problem. He's a little *too* sharp.

You stop walking and think, *What's in the frame of Andrew's car? Safe from what?* Andrew's Rolls is in forward hold No. 2, way down on G Deck near the bow. You're headed that way.

If you postpone meeting Jack to explore Andrew's car, turn to page 64.

If you go to meet Jack with the binoculars, turn to page 93.

Over the next few days, you and Jack Hard-castle explore the ship. It's like an immense, fancy floating hotel. There's a Turkish bath, a swimming pool, a squash court, a gymnasium, a barbershop, a hospital, a post office, and several restaurants and cafés.

Late Sunday evening, about eleven-thirty, you and Jack are in the first-class lounge on A Deck. You've been there for a couple of hours playing cards. Abruptly, Jack puts his cards down.

"I'm bloody bored playing gin rummy." He folds his arms and looks disgruntled. Jack is bright and generally agreeable, but he's a little spoiled.

"Let's go out on deck and see what's going on up forward," you suggest. You're getting bored playing cards in the lounge too.

"Same ocean up there that's back here," he says grumpily.

"Then how about the Marconi Room where the radio transmitter is?" you ask. "I know one of the men who operates the radio there. Wait'll you see it—it's huge!"

*Turn to page 6.*

# 12

You push through the people in the staircase foyer to the port boat deck. It looks empty; then you hear voices over the rail. You lean over it and look. They're loading another lifeboat, No. 4, from the deck below, A Deck. You go down and watch. The *Titanic* has listed so far to port that the lifeboat has swung clear of her side by several feet. Soon you're helping pile deck chairs across the gap to make a flimsy bridge to the lifeboat. You help a man across: You hand him up, then steady his legs as he teeters over.

*Crack!* You hear a gunshot from the starboard side!

*Turn to page 85.*

"It's gold!" you exclaim.

"Gold! What's Andrew doing with gold hidden in his car?" asks Jack.

"I think I know," you reply. "I think the gold is my father's. We'd better get the other one out and take them with us."

"But what will we do with them?" asks Jack. "And what do you mean, you think the gold belongs to your father?"

"I'll explain later. Help me get the other one out. I don't think Andrew will bother checking the car before the ship docks." You're sure the bars are the gold statues. Andrew probably replaced the real statues with lead counterfeits, then melted the originals down into these ingots. Now he's trying to smuggle them into the United States. And somehow Oscar's involved in this scam.

*Turn to page 30.*

You zip down the stairs to the stateroom you're sharing with Andrew. It's on B Deck, a couple of decks below on the port side. As you reach your cabin door, you hear a loud voice inside: "... safest there, I tell you! No one will think of a car's frame—" The voice stops short as you knock a couple of times and enter.

Andrew is talking to a dark-haired man. They both look at you sharply. "Sorry, just want to get these," you say. You grab the binoculars from the table and leave.

As soon as you're outside, you grimace with disgust. The man is Oscar Kilpatrick, a friend of Andrew's. He got on the *Titanic* at Queenstown, Ireland, on Thursday afternoon. You don't like him. When he boarded, he greeted Andrew but ignored your offer to shake his hand.

*Turn to page 10.*

# 16

"We're building a raft. There aren't enough lifeboats, sir," says McCracken.

"Lifeboats! What? No one's told me anything. However, that's ship's property you're using. You're unauthorized to do that," he says. He looks angry.

"Call the bridge, sir," you shout up to him. "We hit an iceberg an hour ago. Look—there's a lifeboat."

You point to the starboard side of the well deck. A lifeboat drifts slowly astern, illuminated by blazing lights from the *Titanic*'s upper decks.

"My God," says the quartermaster, and picks up the aft bridge telephone. A moment later he rushes off the bridge, goes below, and disappears forward carrying a metal case.

"Communication could be better on this ship," says McCracken.

"Well, what we have to figure out now is how to get this monster over the side without smashing it or having it fall into the water upside down," you say.

McCracken, Andrew, and you fit empty wooden barrels under the platform and lash them on with rope passed through some metal rings Andrew found in the workshop.

"Nothing says we can't use that cargo crane up there," says McCracken. "It's the latest thing. Run by electricity." He points to one of the cranes near the raft. Its hook hangs high above you.

*Go on to the next page.*

"Can you run it?" you ask.

"My bunkmate's the one who runs it. I've watched him," says McCracken.

You wonder about the wisdom of getting the raft into the water by using the crane. It's risky. Running the crane may draw too much attention to your project and someone could interfere.

You could just wait and let the *Titanic* sink out from under the raft. But the ship could take such an angle as she sinks that the raft might get tangled or mashed against something on deck.

*If you ask McCracken to run the crane,*
*turn to page 42.*

*If you decide to wait and let the raft*
*float free from the ship naturally,*
*turn to page 78.*

## 18

The water rises to one of the open portholes in front of you and flows inside in a silver cascade.

"Jack, see if you can find your father. We have to unhook the raft soon!" you call. He takes off.

Along with McCracken, a bunch of people appear at the rail, some holding children. "Come on," you motion to them.

Jack slides down with his father and says, "My mother got off in a boat. Andrew's brought a friend."

At the rail Oscar Kilpatrick is motioning to you. He and Andrew are holding a fat leather satchel with a line tied around it, which they have begun lowering to you.

*Turn to page 76.*

"What's in the case?" you gasp, as you plunk your end down on the bridge deck.

"Rockets," he answers. "Bigger than the ones they use for your Independence Day. Distress signals to ships in the area. See those lights? They're masthead lights on a steamer standing off from us."

You watch the officer unload the rockets, then you help set a long rocket in a launching shoot. The officer fits a detonator to it.

"Stand clear; hold your ears," he says, and pulls the firing cord.

The thunder of the rocket's launching detonator smacks your ears. *Tadoom!* The blinding blue-white light of the explosion illuminates startled faces further aft by the lifeboats. A delicate arc of white sparks traces the rocket's path above the *Titanic*. It explodes with a bass *boom* and a white flash. Smaller clusters of blazing white lights drift to the sea.

"Wow, that *is* better than the Fourth of July!" you say.

"Got any colored ones?" a voice comes from the stairway.

"Jack! Come here," you yell. "Look at the ship's lights. We're trying to signal her."

*Turn to page 102.*

A sigh seems to go up from the water surrounding the sinking ship. It's echoed by gasps from the lifeboats standing by.

A shouting, crying chorus of voices swells louder and louder as the ship disappears and darkness returns.

"Oh Lord, it's people in the water," a voice says behind you.

"They look like floating seagulls," another says.

"It's their white life belts," you say. "Let's see if we can rescue some of them. We're only half full."

"They'll freeze to death in this water in a half hour or less," says one of the crew members. "But there aren't enough lifeboats for everybody."

"They'll swamp our boat," shouts a passenger. "Then we'll all die, freezing in that water!"

*Turn to page 54.*

"Even if Alexander and Oscar check the car and find the gold missing, there's no reason they would suspect us," you reassure Jack. "Besides, once the ship docks, we may never get another chance to get the gold."

You and Jack each take a bar and slip it under your jacket.

"We can't risk hiding them in our cabins. Let's stash them in one of the lifeboats," you say.

It's difficult keeping the heavy bar hidden under your jacket as you ascend the spiral staircase. You climb three more flights to reach the boat deck where the lifeboats are located. It's on a level with the bridge. A short distance down the deck you see a figure emerge from a doorway.

"Quick!" you whisper to Jack. "We've got to dump this gold." You shove the ingots under the canvas covering of the lifeboat nearest you.

"Hey there!" says the man. You recognize the voice—it's Oscar! "What are you two doing here? I thought you'd gone to bed."

"We decided to stroll around the ship first," you say, trying to sound nonchalant.

"Why're you hanging around the lifeboats?" Oscar asks. He sounds suspicious.

"We were just checking out the davits, to see how they work," you say. "Well, we're going to turn in. See you later." You hurry away with Jack.

*Go on to the next page.*

"Phew, that was close!" you say to Jack when you're out of Oscar's earshot.

"Do you think he saw the ingots?" asks Jack.

"No, it was too dark," you say, with more confidence than you feel.

"How are we going to get the gold when the ship docks tomorrow?" asks Jack.

"When the first-class passengers are lining up to disembark, meet me by the lifeboat with a small carrying case," you say. "We'll each carry off an ingot as part of our luggage. Just be sure not to let anyone touch your case."

Everything goes as planned. There is just one moment of panic when Oscar offers to carry your case, but you insist on carrying it yourself. You just hope you haven't aroused his suspicions by being too insistent.

*Turn to page 71.*

# 24

Wearily you open the door. You explain that you are exhausted, you don't want any money, you have a concert to do in a couple of days, and the only thing you want is some peace and quiet.

After you give them a statement about the *Titanic,* they finally leave you alone.

## The End

"Yes, I can use your help, Mr. McCracken," you say. "Come on." On the way to your stateroom you hear a voice boom, "Women and children in the boats first, please." It sounds like it's coming through a megaphone way up forward.

"Hey, where have you been? Scrounging bread at a time like this? Don't mind if I have a piece, do you?" asks Jack. He and Andrew are standing just outside the stateroom door. You introduce McCracken to them and outline your plan.

Jack says he'll help with the raft. His folks have gone up to the lifeboats.

Andrew, up and dressed now, says, "I've checked with one of the ship's officers. You're right—it's women and children first, and there aren't enough lifeboats. I'm for the raft. I don't think the *Titanic* will sink, but just in case. No one can live long in the North Atlantic. That freezing water is certain death."

*Turn to page 49.*

"Let's wait it out. The water's almost here," you say. McCracken shrugs but nods his agreement.

The *Titanic*'s bow is now underwater. She's slipping forward and down into the sea. The angle is getting steeper.

The raft leans against the increasingly steep angle of the well deck. Off both sides of the stern, lifeboats move slowly away from the *Titanic;* in her bright lights they glow white against the smooth black water. The people in the lifeboats appear to be having trouble rowing.

"Doesn't the *Titanic* have crew who know how to row?" you ask McCracken.

"Reckon there's a few boatmen, but I'm sure none of 'em made it into that boat," he says.

Freezing cold water swirls over your feet, bringing you both back to reality.

"Wow, cold!" you shout. "McCracken, we've got to get this raft over now! Can you find help? Maybe there are some people still down in third class. Tell them all the lifeboats are gone."

McCracken scrambles up the deck and disappears into the third-class entrance.

A moment later, a crowd pours out of the entrance; some are brave enough to slide down to the raft.

"No one told us! We didn't know the ship was sinking."

*Turn to page 77.*

You plunge in after Jack and grab his life belt. For a moment you keep him from being sucked through the window into the sinking ship. Then you have to let go, and you're sucked in too.

**The End**

"But the bars are too heavy to carry easily," protests Jack. "And what if Oscar or Andrew *does* decide to check the car? We could be in big trouble."

He's right. The bars *are* heavy, and you're not sure where to hide them. On the other hand, few people are wandering around this late at night; no one is likely to see you. You need just ten minutes or less to get the bars out of the hold and into a safe place abovedecks.

*If you take the gold ingots out of the car hold, turn to page 22.*

*If you leave the gold in the Rolls, turn to page 89.*

Instantly Andrew is kneeling down, peering under the car. "What? Who's there? What are you doing under my car?"

You're still holding the gold ingot. You'll have to tell him the truth.

You tell him about the conversation you overheard between him and Oscar but leave out the part about your suspicions concerning the gold Buddha statues.

"I was just curious to find out what was in your car," you say. "I was trying to get the gold back in the frame when you came in."

Andrew looks at you coolly for a moment. "Okay," he finally says. "I believe you. But I better not catch you snooping around this hold again. And you better not breathe a word of this to anyone, or you might just have an unfortunate accident. Do you get my meaning?"

You nod vigorously.

"I'll be watching you," he adds as you and Jack leave the hold.

You still hope to get a message back to your father about the gold once the ship docks in New York. But it's going to be difficult with Andrew and Oscar watching your every move.

**The End**

# 32

"Take it easy, take it easy," you say, moving slowly toward the boat.

"Don't shoot the poor men!" says a girl in the lifeboat. She starts to cry. People standing around begin murmuring; it encourages you.

Staying out of Murdoch's line of fire, you take a slow step toward the two men. You try to keep a calm tone in your voice. "Look, there's another collapsible boat up on the roof of the officers' quarters," you say and point to it.

Never mind that it will be impossible to get it down and launch it before the deck itself dips under the approaching water.

Without a word, the men begin to move. Murdoch pockets his revolver. Several men rush to the boat, grab the two stowaways, and drag them out.

Murdoch motions to you and says, "Thanks. What are you doing here? Thought I sent you off in a boat half an hour ago."

"There's plenty of time left, sir," you say.

"Mind checking steerage—third class?" he asks. "Bring up any women and children left. We'll work on getting that collapsible up there launched by the time you return. Better hurry."

You find a group of young people at the front of the main third-class staircase under the poop deck. But by the time you persuade a few of them to join you, the *Titanic* has begun her slide beneath the sea. A pocket of air remains in the stairway for several minutes as the ship accelerates toward the bottom.

**The End**

You never forget the eerily calm night the *Titanic* sank. You don't forget the sounds the helpless people in the water made. Of the eighteen lifeboats that were launched that night, only your lifeboat and one other went back to help. The others, most of them with extra room, just rested their oars.

**The End**

You stay calm, fascinated by the spectacle of the great ship's stern blocking the stars.

"Let's paddle, all together. Go!" you say. The raft moves a few feet from the ship's vertical side. The *Titanic* is sinking so slowly and evenly there's only a ring of white foam encircling her to mark her motion. Clusters of people cling to the ship, then drop off into the sea, screaming. Only a few make it to the raft.

"Look at that fellow," Jack says. A man is calmly picking his way onto the stern plates as they rise. He's balancing himself perfectly, standing straight up above the stern railing. Always finding the level, he rides the stern straight down out of the night sky. The stern disappears with a gurgling sound and the man calmly steps off into the water as though he were getting out of an elevator.

"It's the chief baker," you say, and throw him a rope. You pull him up onto the raft.

He recognizes you. "Sorry I didn't bring any bread. But I do have this." He reaches into his hip pocket and passes around a flask of brandy.

Shortly after dawn, a ship picks you up. Andrew and his friend give you a check for five thousand dollars later that day. You use it to buy the grand piano of your dreams.

**The End**

"But ma'am, we're in danger. The ship's badly damaged. You should get topside. Captain's order—for your safety," you say.

"Who are you? Leave us alone, or I'll call our steward," a man's deep voice shouts.

"Just don't ask him to mop up the seawater when it starts pouring into your room," you snap back.

You head back up to the boat deck. From the A Deck lounge, lively music, a ragtime number, pours out along the promenade. *What's going on now on this crazy ship?* you wonder as you poke your head in.

Men, women, and children are moving restlessly around like a crowd after a school football game. No one's paying attention to the band or their music.

The band takes a break, and you tell the piano player how serious the damage to the *Titanic* is.

He shrugs and says, "Best to keep playing. Keeps me busy, you know. Maybe she won't sink anyway."

When you reach the boat deck again, many more people are there, and they look more serious and nervous than the group who got into lifeboats earlier. Almost all wear life belts.

*Go on to the next page.*

You begin helping women into one of the lifeboats. Some refuse to leave their husbands and remain on deck.

"Go ahead, dear. I hear several ships are coming soon to take the rest of us. You must get in," says a man to his wife.

You stand in the lifeboat to help those who are having a hard time crossing the gap between the ship and the boat.

A man pushes through the crowd to hand you a folded piece of paper. Then he's roughly yanked back.

*Turn to page 106.*

"Okay, kid, where's the gold?" Oscar growls. "And don't play dumb. I know you've got it here."

You nod to Jack, who opens his case, revealing the bar of gold. Oscar immediately strides over to examine it. For a moment, he stands with his back to you, ignoring you. You creep up behind him with your case containing the other ingot and, with all your strength, strike him on the back of the head.

He instantly crumples to the floor.

"Time to call the police," you say to Jack, "and explain everything."

Andrew and Oscar are arrested for grand larceny. You receive commendation for your role in saving the *Titanic* and for your brave actions leading to the arrest of the criminals. Best of all, your father agrees to split the profits from the sale of the gold with you, and you are able to buy the grand piano of your dreams!

**The End**

# 40

It's so dark. You didn't plan on the lights going out! Icy water swirls around your feet.

You yelp at the shock of the cold, then shout, "McCracken, cut her loose! I can't find my knife. I think the ship's going down!"

You glimpse the dim shapes of bodies falling. Several people have slid down the well deck and bumped up against the raft.

"I can't," yells McCracken. "Someone knocked my knife out of my hand. Jump for it!" He wades away along the horizontal well deck bulkhead.

You don't let go. The stern is pointing straight up in the air; the water is up to your knees. A calm comes over you now that the water has reached you. Maybe you're just numb. You want to try untying the raft, even though it seems useless. You've got just seconds to act.

*If you swim for your life,*
*turn to page 46.*

*If you try to untie the raft in the rising water,*
*turn to page 72.*

You and McCracken motion to the men to lift the raft over the rail. The two of you loop lines tied to the raft around the railing and try to lower it gently to the water.

The raft swings away from you; your left hand is crushed between the railing and the line. You jump into the water to get to the raft, which has landed intact. Some people follow; some cling in fear to the sinking ship.

Late the next morning, the surgeon onboard the SS *Carpathia,* which has picked up you and the other *Titanic* survivors, tells you your hand will heal, but you'll never play the piano again. Your brilliant musical career has ended, but at least you're alive.

**The End**

# 42

"Okay, let's hoist her," you say. McCracken releases the crane's storage tie-downs. Jack rigs some lines from each corner of the raft to meet over its center.

McCracken swings the cargo crane over the raft. All you hear is the whirr of its gears; the electric motor is quiet. He lowers the crane's boom and poises it over the raft. Jack grabs the hook and loops the lines over it.

"Take her up," you yell, and jump onto the raft. You steady yourself by grabbing the lines that come together in a pyramid above your head.

You're afraid the whole thing will tip and dump you. But McCracken is smooth, and miraculously the raft lifts, levels, and gently descends clear of the *Titanic*'s side. The lit portholes blink by you as you glide gently onto the water.

"Hold it! Perfect!" you shout up to McCracken. "Slide down the lines. The *Titanic*'s sinking fast!"

*Turn to page 18.*

"Jack, tonight's the night to explore Andrew's car," you say outside the dining room. "We may dock tomorrow night. Besides, Andrew and Oscar look too drunk to do anything but go to bed."

"I'm ready," says Jack. He slips back to his folks' cabin to get their new battery-powered light.

You meet Jack at the forecastle entrance and descend the spiral staircase to the car hold, five decks below the entrance. It's quiet in the hold, with only the steady hum of the ship's engines vibrating the deck.

You locate Andrew's black Rolls-Royce and, with the help of Jack's flashlight and the car's tool kit, explore the frame. On the driver's side you discover two oblong objects wrapped in white cloth. You manage to slide one out of the frame. It lands on the wood deck with a dull thud. Jack pulls the wrapping off to reveal a gleaming metal bar.

*Turn to page 13.*

"I'd like to get it back to my father, some-how," you say. "Or at least let him know that Andrew's cheating him."

"Well," says Jack, "we could go back to the car and get the gold out. I'd like to see those gold bricks!"

"Yes, but I don't want to draw attention to ourselves," you say. "I don't want Andrew or Oscar getting suspicious. Anyway, this iceberg hit seems kind of serious. Why are we stopped?"

The *Titanic* is motionless. Passengers up on the promenade deck walk along arm in arm, talking and laughing and pointing at the ice in the well deck where you're standing. Two girls are having a snowball fight with chunks of ice. Plumes of steam rise high above the resting ship.

The roar of escaping steam sounds ominous, as though the ship were in pain. What should you do?

*If you return to the car with Jack, turn to page 58.*

*If you ask Jack to explore aft along the passenger decks with you, turn to page 108.*

# 46

The water is now too deep for wading over the well deck bulkhead, so you just swim for it, away from the foundering stern. You breathe in short gasps, the icy air stinging your lungs, the cold water cramping your body. You're too scared to look back at the *Titanic*'s immense sinking hulk.

In the dim starlight, something looms out of the smooth black water. With already numb fingers, you reach for it, gasping from the cold. It's a bunch of deck chairs, still in a nested stack. By crawling on them and balancing carefully, you manage to keep most of your body out of the freezing water. You have to lie perfectly still to keep your balance. The sea remains calm and smooth.

After a while, you can no longer hear the shouts and cries of people in life belts around you. You're not sure whether they've fallen silent or whether you are just drifting into unconsciousness. It makes no difference to you.

A lifeboat appears and voices call. You struggle to raise your head. Strong hands hoist you into the boat. In a miraculous recovery, after a couple of minutes of shaking your legs and waving your arms, you feel strong enough to help row.

**The End**

"Let's go back, Jack," you say.

You tell the captain to get someone else to fire the rockets. Then you and Jack head for the boat deck.

The deck's angle is steep, and the people crowding it are wearing life belts. They look worried—kids holding on to their mothers, some people getting in boats, some holding back and clinging to each other.

"I've got to find my folks!" Jack says. He finds his steward on deck and asks about them; the steward thinks they left in a boat. Your steward says the same about Andrew.

"What do we do now?" asks Jack. You're standing by the starboard rail, watching the last boat leave.

The *Titanic* is clearly doomed. The water is about ten feet from the rail. Far forward near the bow, the last of the forecastle has sunk, its lights glowing green through the water.

"Let's jump and swim to those lifeboats," you say, pointing to several boats visible on the smooth water. The stars twinkle on its surface.

"No. I can't swim that well," Jack says. "Let's wait."

You say nothing. The sea starts pouring into the deck below through the observation windows.

"Okay, now," says Jack.

"Wait!" you yell, and grab at him. He falls into the water alongside the ship. It swirls in a whirlpool as it sluices through the windows.

*Turn to page 29.*

It takes you, Andrew, Jack, and McCracken half an hour to haul a pile of planks, hammers, nails, and barrels for flotation up to the aft well deck. It's the best place to build a raft—the *Titanic* is sinking bow first. The aft well deck is open, near the supplies, and a good location to launch the raft from. The *Titanic*'s bow is noticeably down now, and the well deck is slowly tipping to one side.

"She's listing to port now," Jack says. He nails a large platform of planks he's laid out to four cross timbers.

"Everyone's below decks back here," you say. "It's weird."

"What's going on down there?" says a loud voice from the aft bridge that runs along the poop deck in the stern. It's the quartermaster.

*Turn to page 16.*

# 50

The order is given; crewmen on the deck pull on lines, and the lifeboat swings out on its davits clear of the *Titanic* in a series of alarming jerks. Crewmen struggle to lower the bow and stern fall lines evenly to the water, but it's hard to do. Once you all have to shout up to them to stop lowering the bow fall line—the lifeboat's bow is tipping so low that everyone starts screaming and scrambling to hold on.

On the water, you start to pull on one of the four oars. It's hard work. No one is used to such a large, open boat. She is supposed to hold about sixty-five people, but the boat's only half full.

"Hold the blade of the oar like this." You show a young woman sitting across from you.

"Thanks. I'm just so nervous!" she says. "Do you think the *Titanic* is really going to sink?"

A sharp explosion rips over the still waters. From the bridge a white rocket sails up and arcs through the night. It detonates with a boom and sends out a cluster of white twinkling stars.

*Turn to page 117.*

## 52

You start shouting. Soon many voices take up the chant. "Stop lowering!" Other voices merge in, trying to name the descending boat's number. Different voices call out different numbers. All is confusion.

A crewman tries to cut the fall lines. Another tries to push the boat away from the ship with an oar.

People are screaming in both boats just before they collide. Your boat is crushed and shoved underwater.

### The End

You decide to stick with setting off the rockets. Many lives may depend on you now.

Jack sets a rocket in its launcher, you fix the detonator on it, he keeps track of the five-minute interval, and you pull the cord that fires the detonator.

That ship should have responded by now to the rockets and the Morse light Jack's flashing into the night. So far, it shows no sign that it's seen the *Titanic*'s signals. You crack another Fourth of July joke to keep down the panic welling inside you.

**The End**

# 54

"We can't just leave them to die in that freezing water," says a woman at an oar beside you.

"Let's row," you say. The two of you start, and the seaman at the tiller turns the boat toward the mass of people in the water yelling for help. The other two people at the oars refuse to row at first, then make feeble rowing motions. But it's easy to cover the six hundred yards back to the floating survivors.

It's scary; there are so many people in the water. There must be hundreds and hundreds, you think. As you near the struggling bodies, you worry about the boat being swamped with those trying to climb aboard. But people are so frozen after a few minutes in the water, they have no strength to hold on to the boat, much less swamp it. In fact, it's exhausting work trying to get a full load of swimmers over the three-foot-high sides of the lifeboat. Their soaked clothes and bulky life belts make it slow going.

Most of the rescued lie in the bottom of the lifeboat, moaning. Some are very still and appear frozen.

At last, someone on your boat begins to row toward the other lifeboats. You and the seamen are worn out from the work. Dawn is breaking; a wind begins to blow.

A shout goes up from some boats in the distance. Your binoculars show a steamer making speed in your direction. She's sending up rockets to show she's seen you. Rescue!

*Turn to page 33.*

"Okay," you say, and grab a handle. Together you slide the case up the stairs and carry it to the open part of the bridge. The heavy case reminds you of the hidden gold. You leave the bridge and cut a message with your knife in the soft brass metal of the plaque on the door to the stairway. Above and below the words THIS DOOR FOR USE OF CREW ONLY, you carve GOLD IN ROLLS-ROYCE IN HOLD, APRIL 15, 1912.

You rush over to the other side of the boat deck, hoping no one saw you. What if the *Titanic* doesn't sink and someone finds the message?

You're engulfed by frightened passengers, shouting officers, and sweating crew. You work your way through the crowd. It surges aft till you're by lifeboat No. 13. You wonder if Jack's near and push closer to the boat.

"Let go of me! I won't go in that boat. Let go," says one woman.

"Lady," says a steward trying to help her, "we all have to go. You may as well go quietly."

The woman pulls away, pushes back to the first-class staircase, and disappears.

Beside you, a girl who's been looking over the *Titanic*'s rail at a lifeboat descending to the water begins to cry.

*Go on to the next page.*

"My mother's in that boat. I didn't have time to get in," she says, turning to you.

You grab her hand, push through to the officer loading No. 13, and explain.

"Get in now," he yells to you both.

As soon as you scramble into the boat, it begins to descend to the water.

Directly in the lifeboat's path, about twenty feet below the rail, a spout of water three feet in diameter foams from the *Titanic*'s side!

*Turn to page 97.*

# 58

As you and Jack enter the forecastle spiral staircase, a rat scurries out the door onto the deck and vanishes behind a capstan.

"Where's the car?" asks Jack.

"On G Deck, I think. But look! It's too late—it's partly underwater." You wade along the passageway on G Deck to the car hold. Icy water curls around your knees. The door won't budge.

"Hey, give us a hand saving the mail," a voice calls out from further down the passageway. A group of postal clerks beckons to you.

"We hauled all the sacks up from the deck below to this sorting room," one of them says. "Now *this* deck's flooding. Wish they'd get those pumps working."

"Here, help us with these," says another clerk to you and Jack.

You make a trip up to F Deck carrying the heavy mail sacks, and hurry back down to G. You run into the mail sorting room and slosh toward the last dry bag of mail on the table. The overhead lights are steady and bright. It's so strange to see important letters and packages floating around!

A crumping sound rumbles through the room. The ship's bow drops lower in a sudden motion.

"Watch out!" cries Jack behind you.

A wall of water and heavy wet mailbags slams into you, forcing the door shut and pinning you to the floor. By the time Jack and two clerks work the door open and drag you up for air, it's too late.

**The End**

You and McCracken tie the raft to a couple of rings set in the wood deck for holding deck cargo.

The *Titanic* lurches forward into the water. The horrendous sound of heavy metal tearing apart rises from beneath you in the hold. The deck shudders under your feet. Muffled snapping sounds boom from inside the ship.

"There she goes," shouts McCracken. "Sounds like she's breaking in half!"

*Turn to page 70.*

You have to save the gold! This could be your only chance. You push open the car hold door.

You kneel down by the Rolls. It takes you a couple of minutes to unbolt the plate and pull one gold bar from underneath the car. You set it on the front seat. The bars weigh so much you can only carry one.

Wham! Something smacks the back of your head.

You awake slumped in the car's front seat. Your head is throbbing. The gold is gone. Your knees are being lapped by icy cold, foamy sea-water.

Holding your head, you stand up slowly and swish through the numbing water to the door. It's locked. You pound and pound and yell for help until you're hoarse. No one comes.

The water is up to your waist now and still rising. You climb onto the roof of the car. Was the door locked on purpose to help save the ship from flooding, or to keep *you* in? You wonder as you wait and the water continues to rise.

**The End**

# 62

You feel numb. You can't believe that this wonder ship is going to sink. She feels like a rock under your feet. She's so big, and the sea's so calm.

But as you walk down a couple of decks and aft toward Jack's cabin, you know it's true: the *Titanic* is sinking. What can you do if there really aren't enough lifeboats? An idea pops into your mind. You recall now who that man with Captain Smith is. He's the ship's engineer. He showed you around the ship's workshop. You saw lots of carpentry supplies—planks, rope, and barrels. With help, you could build a decent raft in under an hour.

Outside Jack's cabin you feel a flutter of panic. He's not there. Maybe there's no time to build the raft, and you should just concentrate on finding your friend.

*If you look for Jack in the Marconi Room up on the boat deck, turn to page 79.*

*If you head for the workshop to start building the raft, turn to page 73.*

The *Titanic* limps at half speed into New York, two days late. Damage below the starboard waterline has kept all her pumps working continuously. Hull plates on three of her forward watertight compartments are badly smashed by the brush with the iceberg.

Your steward saves a great chunk of ice in the ship's refrigerated storage for you. You show it to the *New York Times* reporter after the *Titanic* docks. You and your ice end up in a front-page picture.

**The End**

# 64

You hurry to the forward well deck, which shelters you from the icy air, and cross to the forecastle entrance up near the bow. You descend a steep spiral stairway and reach the car hold, five decks below the forecastle entrance.

Inside the hold it's quiet and smells of motors. Light gleams off the black Rolls-Royce. Thick ropes around each axle anchor the car securely to the hold deck. You look around. No one else is there.

You explore the car's frame. It consists of large, pipelike tubes. On the driver's side you spot a metal end plate that seals one of the hollow tubes. You find a wrench in the car's tool kit, remove the bolts, and pull the plate off. You strain to see inside. It's too dark. You light a match. The flame shows something that doesn't belong there.

Before the match dies, you barely make out two rectangular objects wrapped in white cloth. With a wire you manage to hook one bundle and gently tug it up the frame tube. It falls onto the deck with a dull thud. Some of the cloth rips away.

The next match you light shows a bar of shiny metal almost a foot long. "Gold!" you whisper to yourself. "It's a gold ingot!"

*Turn to page 82.*

# 66

The next evening, you're sitting at the captain's table as a guest of honor along with Andrew and your friend Jack. The table is in a recessed bay of the huge first-class dining room. The room is beautiful, with splendid white walls and a molded ceiling.

The captain is an old, white-haired man with a mustache. His voice is soft, low, and reassuring. Also at the table is a quiet man, Mr. Ismay, head of the White Star Line. He and the captain have promised you a special tour of the *Titanic* from stem to stern, all decks, with an engineer to answer your questions about the superpowerful steam engines.

The whole evening seems unreal. But soon you and Jack become bored with the polite conversation. You've got something else on your mind anyway: the mystery of what's in Andrew's car.

This has been bothering you ever since you overheard Andrew and Oscar's conversation. Whatever it is, you suspect it's illegal. Andrew seems nervous. He's drinking too much and talking loudly to Mr. Ismay about a shipment of his and your father's.

*Go on to the next page.*

Over at another table you see Oscar Kilpatrick. It looks like he's had his share to drink tonight too. Dinner's over. You're trying to figure out the best way to get a look at that car. First you have to find out something.

"Captain, sir, when do you expect us to dock in New York City?" you ask.

"Tuesday evening," he answers. "We're making good time—also thanks to you."

Tuesday evening! That's tomorrow night— earlier than expected. It doesn't give you much time to search the car. During a pause in the conversation, you and Jack politely excuse yourselves and leave.

*Turn to page 43.*

With a yell, you dive away from the upended ship. The freezing water feels like razor blades slashing your skin.

You swim underwater as far as you can and then start to surface. A strong current sucks you back down. It pins you against what feels like wire mesh. An image of a ventilation screen on the deck flashes through your panicked mind. You push away with all your strength; a moment later the water pouring into the ship through the screen pins you against it again.

Just as your lungs feel like they're about to explode, a bubble of warm air puffs through the screen and gently frees you. But it's too late. The ship has pulled you far underwater.

### The End

# 70

To your amazement, the *Titanic*'s stern settles back more levelly. In the silence you hear many voices screaming and shouting.

A mass of people rushes from the third-class entrance aft of the well deck. They cling to the railings, the aft bridge supports, and the poop deck cargo cranes. Some start climbing down into the well deck toward the raft.

Once again the deck tips. Again the stern begins to poke vertically into the sky. The lights flick off, come back on glowing dull red, then die.

*Turn to page 40.*

You and Andrew, and Jack and his father, are staying at the Waldorf Astoria. You arrange to stay with Jack and his father, figuring it's a safer place for you and the gold.

On your first night, Mr. Hardcastle goes to visit a friend. You and Jack stay behind in the hotel room to discuss what to do with the gold.

"I think I should telegram my father and tell him what's happening," you say.

There's a knock at the door. You exchange glances. Neither of you is expecting anyone. The knock is repeated. Cautiously you open the door a crack.

It's Oscar and he's got a pistol! "Let me in and I won't hurt you or your friend," he says. Reluctantly, you let him in.

*Turn to page 39.*

# 72

You grab at the knots above you on the nearly vertical deck as the stern of the *Titanic* pivots under you and rises into the air for her final plunge.

You look up, awestruck. The stern looks like a giant black castle as it towers above you, poking toward the gleaming stars. Something from the poop deck bridge crashes next to you, showering you with an icy spray. The raft rights itself and floats free for a moment. You scramble up onto it.

Frantically you struggle with the knots and get one untied. You grab for the last line that's still tied. The knot jerks tight under your fingers and disappears underwater. The black wall of the stern is gliding straight down alongside the raft—and pulling it and you underwater!

*Turn to page 8.*

On your way to the workshop you decide to stop at the baker's. You might be able to get some provisions for your raft.

You descend the first-class staircase, go through a door, and down more stairs to the vast kitchens on D Deck amidships. The smell of fresh bread starts your mouth watering.

"There aren't enough lifeboats. I'm going to build a raft. Could you spare some bread?" you ask a burly man pulling a batch of bread out of the oven.

"A raft? Sounds a bit far-fetched to me," says the baker. "We're taking this bread up to stock the boats, but I can give you a loaf. Good luck."

As you start to leave with the loaf tucked under your arm, a voice calls out from behind, "Hey, mate, that raft sounds like a good idea to me." You turn to see one of the bakers walking toward you.

"Mind if I join you? It may be the only way out for the likes of us. Name's McCracken," he says. You shake the floury hand he extends to you.

*Turn to page 26.*

You ignore your fear and run up the steps to the topmost deck, where the bridge is. It's called the boat deck, and it's where the lifeboats are. You're in luck. First Officer Murdoch, who let you look at the bridge the other night, is on duty.

"Sir," you say, gasping for breath as you open the door, "iceberg!" You point dead ahead.

Murdoch whips his binoculars up, stares intently for a second, and leaps to the wheelhouse. "Hard a-starboard!" he commands the man at the wheel.

Your heart pounds. From inside the bridge, you watch the dark mass grow distinct through the binoculars. Clear now is the triangular peak that you saw reflecting the starlight; it's getting bigger. Half a minute goes by, and still the *Titanic* hasn't begun to turn. Then two things happen.

*Clang! Clang! Clang!* The bronze bell in the crow's nest rings three times. They've spotted the danger.

And then the ship's bow starts to move slowly to port. You watch it trace a smooth arc against a few low-hanging stars near the horizon. Your mouth opens; the iceberg's tip looks as high as the *Titanic*'s bridge. It seems certain that the ship is going to smash into the looming, glistening mountain of ice.

*Turn to page 83.*

# 76

"Okay, okay, I see you," you call. "Lower away and get down here." The bag is heavy; you're sure some of the gold is in it. For the first time, Oscar acknowledges you with a nod of thanks. He's shaking with fear. Others leap into the water and climb onto the raft.

The raft floats well on the glassy water. You cast off the lines to the hook.

"Let's get out of here," says Jack. "She's going to suck us down with her."

You realize in horror that you have nothing to paddle with. Everyone frantically tries paddling with their hands and feet, but the raft stays glued to the side of the ship.

Something bounces off the raft. Startled, you look up. Towering 150 feet straight above you and tipping over the raft is the *Titanic*'s stern. It's vertical, pointing straight up at the sky.

Everyone's looking up.

"She's going to crush us!"

"Help my daughter!"

"Jump!"

Someone dives in.

*If you jump too,*
*turn to page 69.*

*If you stick with the raft,*
*turn to page 34.*

Several men, some speaking languages you've never heard, lift and slide the raft through the water of the steeply sloping deck. Stupendous grinding, crashing sounds shake the deck beneath you.

To your surprise, the deck suddenly levels off, and the *Titanic*'s stern settles back on the water; at the same time, the water drains from the deck, and the sea is again ten feet beneath the deck rail.

"Look, she floats again!" a man says in an Italian accent. He's grinning.

"She's breaking in two!" yells McCracken. "This stern'll sink like a stone in a couple of minutes."

*Turn to page 41.*

# 78

"I think it's too risky to hoist her," you say. "Let's wait for the ship to sink enough to float her."

Andrew disappears and Jack runs up to the boat deck to see if he can find his folks.

*Ka-boom!* A white distress rocket launches into the sky, leaving a silver tracing line that arcs above the radio antenna wires between the fore and aft masts. It explodes and sends soft white stars of light into the black sky. *That makes six of those,* you think.

"The ship's tilting up so high we can't use the crane now anyway," you say. The stern keeps mounting steadily higher. The well deck forward bulkhead is nearly horizontal as the deck the raft is on rises to vertical.

You and McCracken shift your footing to this bulkhead and get ready to brace the raft and keep it from tipping over until the sea can flow onto the deck and float it.

"Lash the raft to the deck. That'll keep her from flipping over," says McCracken. "We'll cut her loose when she floats free."

*If you agree and help McCracken tie the raft,
turn to page 59.*

*If you tell him, "Let's wait it out;
the water's almost here,"
turn to page 27.*

Jack's not on the boat deck. You stare at your watch. It's twenty minutes past midnight.

You knock on the door to the radio room and push it open. "Hello," you say to the operator. "Did my friend come by?" He shakes his head.

"We've hit an iceberg. It's serious, I think. She's taking a lot of water along the bow," you say.

"Harold, hear that?" the operator shouts. "That bump was an iceberg!"

A curtain inside parts and Harold appears, buttoning up his shirt. "Ho, then there's work for us tonight," he says. "Might have to head back to Belfast for repairs."

The captain steps into the doorway. You quickly move aside. "Send the usual distress signal. Here's our position," he says, and hands over a slip of paper.

"Captain!" You rush to join him as he leaves. "Is it as serious as it looks? It looked bad in the forward cargo hold."

"You're everywhere, aren't you?" he says. "Yes, it's bad. If you want to help, give a hand with loading the lifeboats down there. Women and children first. Under no circumstances suggest the ship is sinking. We may have a panic on our hands. Clear?"

*Turn to page 112.*

You climb atop the officers' quarters and help sling the heavy, awkward collapsible canvas lifeboat down to the boat deck. Someone's propped oars against the wall to make a slide to the deck.

You hold an oar in place. An edge of the boat gouges your shoulder when a man on the roof lets go too soon. You get a bad flesh wound. The boat flops onto the deck with a splat, right side up.

Everyone's hurrying and getting in each other's way. Someone is attaching lines to the launching davits.

"Watch out!" a crewman on the roof yells.

A wave sweeps you and the people rigging the boat away. The *Titanic*'s bridge has just been flooded with water, and the wave tangles you and another guy together underwater. You push free with a kick and pop to the surface. Your life belt is ripped from your body, and the icy water shoots pain through you.

You catch a glimpse of something flat in the water. The ship's lights illuminate it. It's the collapsible you were struggling with. Feebly you get to it and hold on to its wooden rail. It's half filled with water.

With your last bit of strength, you hoist your numb body into the collapsible and lie half in and half out of the water pooled in the bottom of the boat. Maybe a rescue ship will come by soon. You hope so.

**The End**

# 82

What are gold ingots doing in Andrew's car? Then it comes to you. Of course! The gold Buddha statues! These must be the *real* statues. Andrew is the one who swapped the gold statues with counterfeits and then had the original statues melted down into bars. And now he's smuggling them into the United States. The ingots are too big and heavy for you to lug away alone. You decide to replace the gold bar and get abovedecks where you belong.

Then you think you hear someone coming. Your heart beats hard. No one comes. You rewrap the ingot. You kneel, half under the car, stuff the ingot back in the frame, and bolt the plate on.

*Braang!!!* A deafening noise and shock wave reverberate through the car hold. The sound is like a huge steel vault door banging shut—but it lasts longer, tapering off into a series of rending, ripping sounds. A shuddering vibration lifts the car body above you.

*Turn to page 101.*

A few seconds later the bow clears the iceberg, and the *Titanic* surges past it.

"Lord! Narrow shave," the junior officer on the bridge mutters.

Murdoch walks over to you and says, "I shall commend your action to the captain." You're not certain what that means.

"Just luck, I guess," you say, trying to cover up the fact you're breathing hard from excitement and fear. "Should the ship go slower tonight? If there are more icebergs—"

"Thanks. Visibility is excellent tonight. Time for you to leave now. We've work to do," he says with a smile.

As you leave, you overhear him tell a man who's just come on the bridge, "Mr. Olliver, take these glasses to Fleet and Lee in the crow's nest."

*Turn to page 66.*

On the forward starboard boat deck, the last lifeboat is loading. It's smaller than the regular boats, with a plank bottom and canvas sides. Crew members have raised its sides and set it in the davits nearest the bridge.

Officer Murdoch is pointing a revolver at two men crouched in the boat. "Get out. Clear out now," he's shouting at them.

"What's going on?" you whisper to a man in the tense knot of people—all men—on the deck.

"A couple of cowards jumped into the lifeboat," he says. "The officer fired a shot in the air."

The two men in the boat freeze. One of them begins to whimper.

"Come out now or by God I'll shoot you!" Murdoch yells, his face red. You hear him cock the hammer of his revolver.

If you don't act fast, Murdoch will shoot the men.

*If you say something to persuade the men in the lifeboat to get out, turn to page 32.*

*If you hold your breath and watch, turn to page 92.*

"Let's row toward her—look, the *Titanic*'s signaling again," you say. Another rocket booms off the ship's bridge. "That ship's got to notice."

"Right. Let's pull for her then," says the seaman. The one other crewman from the *Titanic* aboard nods. "No one's going to help us but ourselves."

Rowing is hard work, but it keeps you from freezing in the cold air. In fact, you get so hot you give your coat to a shivering man.

"She's not getting any closer," you say, peering through your binoculars at the ship's lights.

A few minutes pass. "I think that steamer is going away," says the seaman. "All I see is her stern light. It's getting fainter."

The lifeboat is now miles from the *Titanic*. About half an hour ago, the *Titanic* stopped sending up distress rockets. It looks like she's moving away, but you know she's sinking. You feel panic thinking she is leaving you all alone. The other people in the lifeboat are full of doubts.

"Let's turn back."

"We should have stayed with the other lifeboats."

"We're lost!"

Everybody's shouting now.

All the lights from the *Titanic* wink out. The strange steamer's lights are fading. It doesn't seem to matter much what you do now.

*Turn to page 118.*

You need some more time. It may be a mirage. Or maybe it's a cloud.

To get a better view you run up the steep stairway leading from the promenade deck to the boat deck. Before you get there, three distinct rings from the lookouts' warning bell tell you they've spotted something.

You see a huge iceberg looming in the darkness ahead, and coming closer. There's a slight, grinding noise as the *Titanic* brushes the iceberg, and then it's over; the iceberg glides swiftly out of sight into the darkness astern. You hear something crash onto a deck below.

You poke at the ice that's down in the well deck, then push the forecastle door open. Maybe you can find out if any water is leaking into the ship near the bow where the berg struck.

It's quiet. The constant humming and jangling vibration of the ship's woodwork and glass fixtures has stopped. That's strange. You peer down the forecastle spiral stairs.

Three or four decks below, a big blond man with a couple of companions starts climbing the stairs. His feet and legs are dripping, and he's carrying his belongings.

"Ship taking water?" you call out.

"Right she is!" he yells up, with a Swedish accent.

*Turn to page 96.*

# 88

"Row, paddle, push—we gotta get out of here," you yell, stumbling over people to get to the fall lines. You hack them apart, and your boat glides clear just as the descending boat splashes into the sea.

Six hours later you're falling asleep in a warm berth on board the SS *Carpathia,* a liner that rescues the *Titanic*'s lifeboats.

The girl has found her mother and Andrew has found you. To your horror, you later learn that as many as 1,500 people have died, most frozen in the sea, Jack among them. You are one of 705 survivors.

Four days later in New York, you're first off the *Carpathia,* thanks to Andrew's connections. A taxi whisks you to the Waldorf Astoria Hotel. It's late at night. You're overwhelmed by the tragedy and excitement of the *Titanic* disaster.

A frantic commotion builds outside your hotel room door. The phone rings. It's the press calling you, pounding on your door.

"Please, I must get an interview."

"Five hundred dollars for five minutes!"

"Open up! We know you're there."

"You're the first to be interviewed!"

*Turn to page 24.*

You decide it's safer to leave the gold where you found it. But it's not as easy to get the gold bar back inside the car's frame as it was to pull it out. While Jack holds the light, you struggle and push. It's an awkward position, and your arms are getting tired.

Then you think you hear footsteps. "What's that?" you whisper to Jack. You can't see from your position under the car.

"Someone's come into the hold," Jack whispers back.

"Quick, turn off the flashlight and crawl under the car!" you whisper.

*Go on to page 90.*

The two of you huddle together under the Rolls-Royce, not daring to breathe.

The footsteps grow louder. A pair of men's shoes stops right next to the Rolls. You recognize Andrew's brown and white wing tips!

You hear him pack his pipe with tobacco, then strike a match and light the pipe. He nonchalantly leans against the Rolls and smokes. *Will this ever end?* you think. Finally he finishes.

You're about to breathe a sigh of relief when Jack makes a noise, trying to stifle a sneeze.

*Turn to page 31.*

# 92

You hesitate, losing the courage to speak up. Murdoch steps toward the two men. One of them crawls under a seat. Sailors drag them both out amid the screams of several women in the boat.

You stand back against the officers' quarters and watch this last lifeboat slip down to the water as the crew plays out her lines through the davit pulleys. Fear floods you.

You go to the rail. The collapsible lifeboat that just went down is floating near the *Titanic;* they're just getting their oars in the water.

Those left on deck are running toward the stern to get away from the water sweeping in at the bow. A few have climbed to the roof of the officers' quarters with Murdoch and are struggling to free the other collapsible boat. It may be your last chance to save yourself.

But you could jump into the water near the lifeboat and hope they'll pick you up. You feel ashamed of that idea, thinking of the men who were dragged from the boat minutes ago. But there are some male passengers in it. Maybe no one will figure out what you're doing.

*If you jump into the sea
and swim to the lifeboat,
turn to page 110.*

*If you stay aboard the* Titanic,
*turn to page 81.*

You decide to let the mystery in Andrew's car go for the moment. No one can leave the ship until she docks in New York in a couple of days, so it can wait.

Jack is squatting behind the promenade deck railing where it curves around the forward section of the ship on the starboard side. You stand under the bridge with a clear view of the crow's nest, and beyond it, the bow. You hand him the binoculars.

"It's beastly cold," he chatters after a couple of minutes. "I can't see any more with these than I can without them. Just smooth black sea. I'm turning in." He hands the binoculars to you and leaves.

For a couple of minutes, you sweep the horizon in front of the *Titanic*. Just as Jack said, there's nothing but darkness. The stars look brighter through the binoculars, though. The great bronze capstans near the bow glint under the stars. You train your gaze on the two lookouts more than thirty feet above you up in the crow's nest. Funny, they don't have binoculars.

You sweep the horizon another time. You catch a point of light that shimmers faintly. It's duller than starlight. Maybe it's a reflection?

*Turn to page 115.*

Near lifeboat No. 3 on the forward starboard boat deck, First Officer Murdoch is talking to Captain Smith. Some men are uncovering the lifeboats. A group of passengers, some with life belts on, stands around.

"Women and children first," says Officer Murdoch as the captain goes off to the bridge. Murdoch stands near a boat and motions the women passengers on while more people slowly appear on the deck from their cabins below. Excitement is in the air—at least *something* is happening. The boat is now half full of women and children. A few men even get in!

"You with the binoculars—know anything about open boats? We're short of crew on No. 7 here. I want to send her down now," Murdoch says, looking at you.

*If you say, "Yes, I do," and step forward, turn to page 116.*

*If you say, "I think I'd do better helping load boats," turn to page 100.*

# 96

A nervous thrill runs through you at his words, then your heart jumps when you see a tumble of bright green seawater foam around the spiral stairway several decks beneath him. The *Titanic* is in trouble.

"Come! We're going to the stern. It's dry there," he shouts. He beckons to you to follow. You've never met this man, but you immediately trust him.

It's a long trek along the E Deck passageway to the stern. The man shows you into the third-class smoking room. Pine paneling covers the walls. Your friend finds the bar closed, so he persuades someone to start playing dance tunes on the piano.

A cluster of men, women, and children swarm into the large room carrying water-soaked baggage; some of the children and women are crying. Your friend and the others laugh at the new group and begin a circle dance around them to try and cheer them up.

*Weird,* you think. *The ship has hit an iceberg! And no one's doing a thing.*

You leave and go forward toward the lifeboats. A crowd of people is gathered in the first-class lounge, laughing and joking. The entire ship's band is even playing some lively ragtime music. *Don't these people know what's going on?* you wonder, really confused.

*Turn to page 95.*

You point to the spout of water and yell, "Watch out!"

With an oar, you try to shove the lifeboat away from the *Titanic*'s side and the flowing water. If it hits your boat, it'll swamp it and dump all of you into the sea below!

"Push clear!" you shout.

Several more people pick up oars and together you shove the boat out enough to clear as it passes the water spout. Your lifeboat lands safely and drifts back along the ship's side in the flow from the spout.

"Look out above!" calls one of the crewmen in the boat as another lifeboat starts to descend. Your boat has drifted into its path. The fall lines that lowered you are still attached to your boat, holding it in position.

*If you yell out, "Stop lowering,"
turn to page 52.*

*If you take your knife
and cut the fall lines free,
turn to page 88.*

# 98

You decide it's safer to stick close to your mother ship. Another rocket goes off from the *Titanic*'s bridge. *That steamer's got to see these distress signals,* you think.

An hour passes. The steamer's lights disappear, and more lifeboats join you in the dark water. Some of them are full; others are only half full. The boats group not far from the *Titanic*, like children afraid to leave a parent. The *Titanic*'s bow steadily sinks under the water; her decks and portholes blaze with lights. She looks like a vast palace that's askew and tipping. All the lifeboats have left the ship now, and masses of people swarm back toward the stern to escape the black water welling up into the ship's submerging decks.

Fascinated, you all watch the horrifying, gradual disappearance of the ship. The entire forward well deck is underwater. Toward the bow you see portholes still gleaming under it. The *Titanic* looks eerily beautiful, like a supernatural sea creature glowing underwater.

*Turn to page 104.*

# 100

"I think I'd do better helping load boats," you tell Officer Murdoch.

"Go below to Decks B and C amidships and tell passengers to put on their life belts and report here to boat deck. Do it calmly; no one must be alarmed. And get one yourself," Murdoch tells you.

Moving quickly along the corridors of B Deck you knock on one stateroom door after another. Some people are awake, but many have gone to bed. It's well after midnight. You keep missing your step, sliding to the left. The ship's beginning to list.

"Hello, hello!" you call out as you stride along the passageway. "First Officer Murdoch wants everyone on the boat deck. Wear your life belts, please. There's been an accident. This is just a precaution."

A man hears you and waits for you outside his door. "I knew something had happened," he says. "This rumbling sound shook me awake, and a moment later some ice tumbled in my open porthole. Look," he says, and shows you a piece.

"Better get up to boat deck, sir, with your life belt," you say. "Please tell your friends."

Down on C Deck, you knock on a door and run through your routine once again. Click! You hear the door lock.

"Go away!" a woman's voice says from behind the door.

*Turn to page 36.*

You scream and cover your head with your hands. But the car body settles back without touching you. Feeling foolish, you roll out from under the car and run to the forecastle stairway.

Did the *Titanic* hit something? The sound came from below. You move down the stairs to explore. Below is another cargo deck. You open the door and see large, neatly stacked cases. You don't know what you're looking for, but you feel a vague dread. You go down to the bottom of the stairs. Now you're at the bottom of the ship. A sign on the door says FIREMEN'S PASSAGE. CREW ONLY.

When you open it, you hear a hissing and gurgling. Water! A man hurries toward you along the passageway from the boiler rooms. Foaming green seawater is rising above the walkway.

Sloshing through the swirling water, the man shouts, "She's taking water clear back to No. 5 boiler room! She's a goner, mate. Better clear out!"

You run up the stairs after him. At the car hold door, you pause. The gold! Should you save it? Or should you get up on deck?

*If you open the car hold door and try to salvage the gold, turn to page 60.*

*If you continue up the stairs to the well deck to find Jack and see what's happening up there, turn to page 113.*

# 102

"Set the next rocket to fire," the officer says to you. "Detonators are over there. Be careful. I'm going to signal that ship with the Morse light."

Jack helps and decodes out loud the message the officer is sending in Morse code. The signaler looks like a winking searchlight.

"Struck iceberg. Have lifeboats ready to take passengers," says Jack, watching the flashes.

A band of curious onlookers has gathered to watch the rocket show. The captain comes and gives an order; the officer turns to you and Jack.

"I'm to take a lifeboat. Carry on with the rockets, one every five minutes," he says, patting you on the back as he leaves.

*Funny,* you think. No one in charge on the whole *Titanic* seems to have a plan for saving the passengers. Now this guy sticks you with his job. The rocket signals are important, you know. But so is your life.

---

*If you leave with Jack and let someone else worry about the rockets, turn to page 47.*

*If you stick with setting off rockets, turn to page 53.*

Steeper and steeper the ship cants downward into the sea. A roar from inside her, like tons of gravel and rocks running down a steel chute, sweeps across the water. Her engines and everything moveable inside—boilers, coal, freight, pianos, furniture—are crashing toward the bow. Her first funnel, then her second, come smashing down into the water in a spray of red sparks and steam. Over half her length is underwater now; higher and steeper her stern rises, glowing with all her lights. Then the lights go out, and you're alone in the dark. Cracking sounds as sharp as cannon shots resound clearly across the water. The *Titanic* breaks in two between the third and fourth funnels and sparks from the tearing, shearing metal dance into the water. The whole forward two-thirds of the ship sinks.

For a few minutes, the aft third of the *Titanic* levels as though it has stopped sinking. In a moment the broken end sinks into the water as well, and the stern points higher and higher until it stands vertical. The words TITANIC LIVERPOOL point straight up to the stars. With hundreds of people clinging to rails, stanchions, and ventilators, the remaining section of the ship descends straight down like a gliding elevator. Gone!

*Turn to page 21.*

"Ahoy, crow's nest!" you cry your loudest. You wonder if "ahoy" is the right word. You shout a couple of times; the rushing air muffles your voice. They can't hear you shouting from the promenade deck.

You rush down two decks to get to the well deck and then run forward till you're almost under the crow's nest mast. But now the crow's nest is way above you.

"Iceberg, iceberg!" you scream up at them. At your shout, one lookout peers intently into the distance, then clangs the warning bell three times and speaks urgently into a telephone.

It seems like an hour goes by. Nothing happens. You can't feel the slightest change in the rhythm of the *Titanic*'s engines or sense the deck move under your feet the way it should when the ship changes course. And because you're down in the forward well deck area, with the forecastle blocking your view, you can't see the iceberg, either.

Just as you sense the turning of the bow under your feet, a shower of ice cascades over the starboard well deck rail. One of the huge pieces brushes you and slides with a *thump* into the stairway you just came down.

*Turn to page 63.*

# 106

You unfold the paper and glance at it:

*Tell my sister Mabel Nappi of*
*New York City. Lost. J. H. Williams*

After the boat you were loading is lowered, you locate the man standing alone and dejected by an empty boat davit. "Better give this to someone else," you say. "I'm here for a while, like you." He looks like the card shark you saw winning Saturday night in the smoking room. You hand back the piece of paper.

It's about half past one in the morning. Most of the lifeboats have left the starboard side of the ship. The band has moved up to the foyer of the Grand Staircase that connects the decks. You notice a couple of the musicians have life belts on now. They're playing louder, too.

You go to the port side to see what's happening over there; maybe more people are getting into boats.

*Turn to page 12.*

"Jack," you say, "water's rising down in the car hold. It's too risky. Let's see if we can find an officer and get some information. Maybe it's serious. Why else would they stop the ship?"

You climb up to the starboard promenade deck. Through the windows of the smoking room you see groups of men laughing and talking. No one's even looking outside. You can't find any officers, so Jack goes to find his family. You stop by your cabin. Andrew's in bed.

"Andrew, you'd better get up!" you say, jostling him awake. "We've hit an iceberg. It doesn't look good. A lot of water is coming in."

"Huh? An iceberg? I didn't feel a thing, and I'm a light sleeper," he says, sitting up on the edge of the bed. "Don't worry. This ship's supposed to be unsinkable."

"Better get ready, just in case," you say. "Maybe you should check with our steward if you can find him. I'll try to find out as much as I can."

You think of going directly to the bridge this time, even though it's not allowed. Your hunch is that the man from the boiler room who told you the *Titanic*'s a goner is right, but no one else seems to know or care.

*Go on to the next page.*

High up on the top deck, the boat deck, is the bridge, the *Titanic*'s command post. It's also where the lifeboats sit. You peer in a window of the enclosed part of the bridge. Captain Smith and another man are examining a blueprint near the half-open window. You stand quietly nearby.

"Well, sir, I give her an hour, an hour and a half at most," says the man, who looks familiar to you.

"I'll order the lifeboats readied," says Captain Smith.

"Lifeboat capacity is about one thousand. There are more than two thousand people aboard," the man says.

"Women and children first is the rule," the captain says. You slip away to avoid running into a man approaching the bridge.

Your hunch was right. The *Titanic* is doomed, and there's not enough lifeboat space for everyone. Your watch says fifteen minutes past midnight. It's been about half an hour since the *Titanic* hit the iceberg.

*Turn to page 62.*

# 110

You jump feet first into the black water. It's a drop of no more than ten feet, but the cold shock is like a blow.

The sound gets the attention of the people in the lifeboat. They stop rowing. You reach them and shout, "Help me!" Someone pulls you in and throws a blanket over you. You shiver on the bottom of the boat.

For years, you fight off the cloud of shame that hangs over you, even though your friends and family tell you it's ridiculous.

**The End**

# 112

"Yessir!" you answer.

An officer struggling up the steep stairs to the bridge with a large metal case calls out to you.

"Give us a hand up these steps. This climb's about finished me," he says.

*If you give him a hand
and continue on to the boats,
turn to page 56.*

*If you give him a hand
and ask what's in the metal case,
turn to page 20.*

You hesitate, your hand on the door. You sense no vibration, none of the humming sounds a powered steamship makes. *The engines must have stopped,* you think. "Stopped, surrounded by ice," was the message that the other ship radioed. Did the *Titanic* hit ice?

You leap up the forecastle stairway to look for Jack. Two crew members hurry down the stairs.

"That iceberg was as tall as the ship."

"Lucky we just nicked it."

"Check the bow compartments and back to the boiler rooms. We may be taking water."

"Not likely. The iceberg just grazed her."

*That's what you think!* you think. *She's taking lots of water.*

On the well deck, the open area between the *Titanic*'s superstructure and the forecastle, you spot Jack. He and some others are playing soccer with a chunk of ice. There must be tons of ice lying in heaps on the well deck.

Jack kicks a big chunk to you. "Where have you been? Where's the binoculars you were going to get? You should have seen that iceberg the ship hit! It was huge!"

"I left the binoculars down below," you say. You pull him aside and tell him about the gold in the Rolls's frame. Jets of steam are blasting out of the escape pipes mounted on the three forward funnels. You guess the ship is releasing pressure in the boilers now that the engines are stopped.

"You don't say!" Jack exclaims. "Gold! What are you going to do about it?"

*Turn to page 44.*

You strain to see. Something massive, even darker than the sea, begins to fill your view. It's an iceberg! The "light" on top must be shiny ice reflecting the starlight.

"Wow!" you mutter. The lookouts are staring right in its direction, but they can't see it without binoculars.

You keep watching as the object gets bigger. Do you dare run up to the bridge, where no passengers are allowed, and warn the officer on duty? Or should you tip off the lookouts and let them deal with it? Maybe you should wait a little to make sure it's really an iceberg.

*If you go directly to the bridge, turn to page 74.*

*If you call to the lookouts, turn to page 105.*

*If you take time to make sure it's an iceberg before going for help, turn to page 87.*

# 116

You step forward. "Yes, I do."

Hands help you up over the rail into lifeboat No. 7. The seaman from the *Titanic* in charge of the boat tells you to stand in the center while he fits the plug—which covers the boat's rainwater drain—into the boat's bottom.

You feel a quick flood of fear; you wish you were back on the ship with all the people and music and bright lights. You peer over the side. It looks like a million feet to the glassy sea below. And you feel funny about being the first to leave. What if it's a false alarm? What about Jack and Andrew?

"It's a long way down, about seventy feet. Not to worry, we'll make it," the seaman says to you.

*Turn to page 50.*

It reminds you of the Fourth of July. You look at your watch. It's 12:45 A.M., an hour since the *Titanic* struck the iceberg.

"That's your answer, miss," the seaman says. "She's signaling for help—*any* help—now."

"Do you suppose they've seen something?" you ask. You stand and scan the horizon with your binoculars.

To the north, you sight some lights. "Look, ship lights!" you shout.

The seaman confirms your find. "Looks like a steamer—two lights, one on her foremast, the other on her main mast. And it looks like she's headed this way."

*If you suggest heading for the ship, turn to page 86.*

*If you want to wait near the well-lit* Titanic *for the ship to come to you, turn to page 98.*

The White Star Line hires several ships to search the sea for bodies. Three weeks later one of these ships finds lifeboat No. 7 still floating, but with no survivors on board.

## The End

## ABOUT THE AUTHOR

**JIM WALLACE** lived for two and a half years in Tokyo, where he wrote and edited English language textbooks. Since returning to the United States, he has worked as a proofreader and freelance editor. He has written other books in the Choose Your Own Adventure series, and lives in Montpelier, Vermont, with his wife, Kate, and young son, Ian.

## ABOUT THE ILLUSTRATOR

**FRANK BOLLE** studied at Pratt Institute. He has worked as an illustrator for many national magazines and now creates and draws cartoons for magazines as well. He has also worked in advertising and children's educational materials and has drawn and collaborated on several newspaper and comic strips, including *Annie*. The Choose Your Own Adventure titles he has illustrated include *Master of Judo, Who Are You?, Last Run, Ninja Cyborg,* and *Tattoo of Death*.